Penny Tunes and Princesses

by Myron Levoy
Pictures by Ezra Jack Keats

Harper & Row, Publishers
New York, Evanston, San Francisco, London

PENNY TUNES AND PRINCESSES

FIRST EDITION

For Debbie and David

Many years ago, when people came to America from the Old World, they often had to sell all their possessions to pay for their passage. Watches and rings, dishes, pans, coats, jackets, and even shoes were sold. And so, when János Ady left for America, he sold his violin.

János was sure he could buy a better violin in America. And he would be rich, for America was the land of plenty, the land of opportunity, the Promised Land. If people loved his playing in the courtyards of Budapest, Hungary, why shouldn't they love it in the courtyards of New York, America? Wasn't music music everywhere, and couldn't his violin laugh and cry and tease and leap like an acrobat? *Igen*, of course. All would be well. He would be *very* rich. And János wept at the beautiful thought.

On his arrival in America, János took a job as a sandwich man in order to earn enough money for a new violin. A sandwich man didn't *make* sandwiches. Rather, he was a sort of living, walking sandwich. He carried a big wooden sign in front and another big advertisement in back, held up by straps over his shoulders. János felt very much like a sausage between two slices of bread, but one must do what one must do. Well, well, he thought, it keeps me out in the fresh air, and I can see everything that's happening. A most healthy job. But if only I had my *hegedü*, my violin.

János walked and walked, for a sandwich man must keep walking if he wants to be paid. But as he walked, he daydreamed of better things.

HIRSCH'S
HAT'S
WILL

He thought of the wonderful life of Rigó Jancsi, the famous Hungarian violinist. Rigó Jancsi had played in the very best restaurants, and everyone had admired him and his fantastic skill. One day a real princess had heard him play and had immediately fallen in love with him. And so Rigó Jancsi married a princess and became so famous that a chocolate cake was named after him. What more could any sane man ask of life? Ah, what wonderful daydreams János had. If only he could buy a *hegedü*, he knew his fortune would be made.

Week after week, János walked between his signboards, with their messages in black lettering. HIRSCH'S HATS WILL HELP YOU

HOLD YOUR HEAD UP HIGH, screamed the sign in front. FLORA'S GYPSY TEAROOM. YOUR FORTUNE READ FREE IN TOTAL PRIVACY, whispered the sign in back. I don't need another hat, thought János, but I do need to know my fortune. Will I ever be able to buy a violin, when I can save only seven cents a week? I should ask Flora.

Flora's Gypsy Tearoom was cool and dark inside, with little red candles on the tables. Flora was dressed in a red-and-yellow gypsy outfit; she had six bracelets on each wrist and rings on every finger. What a lovely gypsy girl, thought János. If she reads my fortune, my fortune will surely be sweet as sugar.

"Ah," said Flora, "I see a cauliflower in your future, sandwich man."

"No *hegedü*?" asked János.

"The tea leaves say cauliflower. Possibly cabbage. Possibly turnip. No *hegedü*. If your fortune comes true, see me. I have a wonderful recipe for cauliflower."

"Is there, maybe, a princess there?" asked János.

"I'm sorry," said Flora. "The tea leaves have not so informed me."

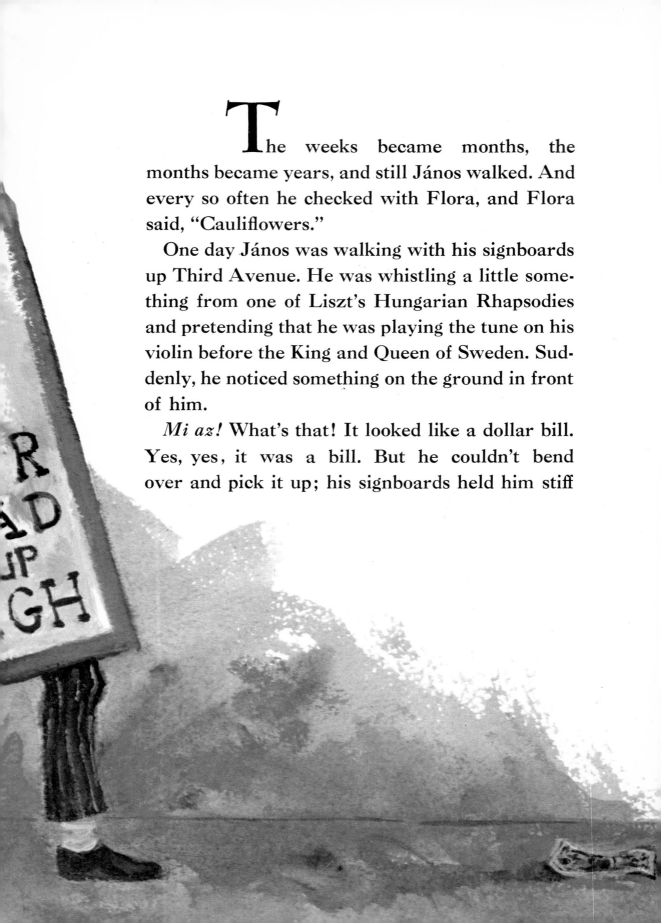

The weeks became months, the months became years, and still János walked. And every so often he checked with Flora, and Flora said, "Cauliflowers."

One day János was walking with his signboards up Third Avenue. He was whistling a little something from one of Liszt's Hungarian Rhapsodies and pretending that he was playing the tune on his violin before the King and Queen of Sweden. Suddenly, he noticed something on the ground in front of him.

Mi az! What's that! It looked like a dollar bill. Yes, yes, it was a bill. But he couldn't bend over and pick it up; his signboards held him stiff as a finger in a splint. So he put his foot over the bill and waited.

In a few minutes, János saw a little boy passing by and called to him, "Ah, young man. I need a favor."

The boy came over and hammered once or twice on the sign, between HIRSCH'S and HATS. "You're wearing a good drum," said the boy.

"If you will be kindly enough to hand me that bill, I will buy you a *real* drum," said János.

And so the boy gave János the bill and János almost fainted. It wasn't a dollar bill, but a *twenty*-dollar bill. Flora, why did you not foresee this miracle!

János went to the nearest pawnshop and bought the boy a drum. Then he selected a beautiful, shiny violin, slender as a cat and as clear of tone as a glass bell. Yes, yes, he thought. Now I shall have my music again, and I shall be rich. I'll turn in my sandwich signs at once.

What a light feeling to walk down the street without those heavy boards. He had been a turtle long enough; now he would be a skylark.

János couldn't wait. He went into a passageway between two tenement buildings, placed his handkerchief on his shoulder, carefully held the violin in place against it, and began.

But wait! What was *this*! In his head, János was playing flawlessly, brilliantly, but what came out of the violin was a discordant jumble of sour notes. Disaster! He hadn't played for over three

years; his fingers no longer felt at home on the fingerboard. They couldn't stretch, they couldn't run, they couldn't leap. Disaster! Absolute disaster!

Then a penny landed at his feet. And another. A voice called down, "Go away! Stop! I'm trying to sleep!" And another voice, "Here's a penny and be *quiet*!" Then a tomato landed near his left foot, and something hard hit him on the head. Disgrace! They were paying him to be quiet. To go. Shame!

They were throwing things at him!

Still, János picked up the pennies. A penny *is* a penny, he had to admit to himself. It would come in handy; he still owed a dollar and twelve cents for the violin. One must make one's way in the world, even in the very face of disaster. Could that tomato possibly be usable? Perhaps the top half. And what was that thing that had just bounced off his head? Aha. A cauliflower. A *cauliflower*! Flora! The tea leaves have told the truth!

János wept as he played in the courtyards and alleys and side streets—wept for his fingers that no longer danced, for the power and perfection that had escaped from him as perfume from an open bottle left standing too long.

But one had to live. And he soon discovered that he was getting more pennies more quickly for bad music in New York than for superb music in Budapest. When he had played well in Hungary, the ladies would listen by their windows for half an hour before they tossed down their *fillérs*, their pennies. But now, they hurled the money at him immediately. And fruit and vegetables, as well.

And though he wept, János was able to earn three dollars a day, which was a great deal, indeed, in those days. He carried a cloth bag at his side into which he popped the best of the tomatoes, onions, cauliflower, beets, and cabbages that bounced around him. He wept as he put them in the bag and wept as he ate them, but he had to confess that, all told, he had never eaten better in his life. Ah, if they would only throw a pot of goulash or a roast chicken.

All the other street musicians envied him. If

only they could play that badly, they told one another, their fortunes would be made. They invited János to join their groups, but János insisted, "No, no. I am, how you say, a soloist. Besides, I play bad, very bad." And he wept as he jingled the pennies in his bulging pockets. "Would you like to buy a fresh cauliflower, very white and sweet?" János asked through his tears. "Or three slightly bruised tomatoes?"

But as the weeks passed, János noticed that it was taking longer and longer and still longer for the pennies to come flying down. There were fewer and fewer onions and beets and carrots hurtling from above. And one day he discovered that he had earned only seventy-eight cents plus one onion and a radish.

Ah ha, thought János. The ladies are no longer chasing me away; they are listening. Through playing every day, my old skill has returned. What joy! The violin has become my friend again.

And indeed the ladies called down, "Beautiful music, violin-man. Play us a love song next! Play us a waltz! Play some more, violin-man!" And János played until his fingers ached.

But then János thought, Oh ho. Soon I will have to play half an hour before they throw me any money. I'm ruined! And János wept bitterly. But even as he wept he realized that one must live in the very teeth of disaster. I'll be poor again, true, but now, at last, I can be proud of my music. I can hold my head up high, even without one of Hirsch's hats. Who knows what may happen. Maybe, someday, I'll play for the King and Queen of Sweden. I'll go to Flora and find out.

Flora studied the leaves at the bottom of his tea-cup and said, "The tea leaves say princess. Possibly duchess. Maybe countess. But probably princess."

János tried to remain calm. "Aren't the tea leaves ever sure?" he asked.

"Never," said Flora.

"Then there maybe is another cauliflower coming?" asked János.

"I'm sorry," said Flora. "The tea leaves have

not so informed me. The message is princess."

A princess! János jumped up, took his violin and played a Hungarian dance, a *czardas*. His fingers flew; his bow flicked in and out like the tongue of a snake. Now I shall be rich, he thought. Rich, rich, *rich*!

And János danced as he played, spinning and swirling and picturing gold coins pouring into piles before his eyes.

Then suddenly János slipped, and the violin crashed to the floor beneath his body. A cracking and splintering of wood and a *ping* of strings snapping were the violin's final song.

"Disaster!" János cried out. "What can I do now! My fortune will never come true!" And again he wept.

"Don't cry, sandwich man," said Flora. "You play a terrific fiddle."

"Thank you," said János, as he wept.

"I am the Princess Flora, who foresees the future and advises. And I advise you to marry me and help me run this tearoom. We'll get another violin. You'll play for the customers, I'll read fortunes as always; and between the two, it's a business. So what do you say?"

Could he believe his ears? Miracle! A real princess! And an offer of marriage! And what's more important, a new *hegedü*! This much happiness

could not occur in so short a time without János weeping again. So he wept, not quite sure whether it was for joy or for sorrow or both.

And so János Ady married Princess Flora, and they lived in a little apartment above their gypsy tearoom on Second Avenue. And more and more customers came to the tearoom to hear the wild gypsy music, which János played as if the strings of his violin were a rainbow, and his fingers a flight of birds.

And János would often think as he played, I am *gazdag*, *gazdag*, rich, rich. I've married a princess, and my *hegedü* has learned to sing like never before. And someday, I'm sure, they'll name a cake after me. It's only a matter of time.